CARTOON NETWORK™

and the SCOOBY-DOO!™
FANTASTIC PUPPET FACTORY

By Jesse Leon McCann

WORLDWIDE PUBLISHING™

SCHOLASTIC INC.

New York   Toronto   London   Auckland   Sydney   Mexico City   New Delhi   Hong Kong

No part of this work may be reproduced, stored in a retrieval system, or transmitted in any form or by any means, electronic, mechanical, photocopying, recording, or otherwise, without written permission of the publisher. For information regarding permission, write to Scholastic Inc., Attention: Permissions Department, 555 Broadway, New York, NY 10012.

ISBN 0-439-17254-3

20   5 6/0

Special thanks to Duendes del Sur for interior illustrations.

Design by Peter Koblish

Printed in the U.S.A.

First Scholastic printing, April 2000

Scooby-Doo and his Mystery, Inc., pals were at the malt shop. Fred and Daphne were getting the gang some goodies while Velma listened to the radio.

"This just in," the radio blared. "The national bank was robbed this evening by the Black Mask Bandits! This is the fifth bank they've hit in a week. The police are baffled."

"Jinkies!" Velma said. "I hope they catch those thieves soon."

"Like, I just hope Fred got us some triple-fudge cheesecake sundaes with extra strawberry sauce on top!" Shaggy said.

"Reah! Reah!" agreed Scooby hungrily.

Just then, the gang was joined by Mrs. Jenkins, a kindly old lady who lived down the street. She looked really worried.

"I'm so glad I found you kids," Mrs. Jenkins said. "Teddy, my poor kitty, is missing. Won't you find him for me?"

"Man, that's the kind of mystery I dig the most — no ghosts, ghoulies, or goblins!" said Shaggy bravely. "Like, don't worry, Mrs. J. We'll find Teddy for you!"

"Oh, thank you!" said Mrs. Jenkins gratefully. "I last saw him in front of that abandoned puppet factory on the corner of Pitman Street."

The gang looked up and down the street for Teddy. As they were searching, they met two security guards, Biff and Bob.

"We were hired to patrol all the buildings on this street," Biff told them. "But we haven't seen any black-and-white cats."

"I'd stay away from that old puppet factory if I were you," said Bob. "We keep hearing strange noises around there, like it's haunted or something."

"H-H-H-Haunted?" Shaggy cried. "Maybe we should look for Teddy somewhere else — like at home in bed, under the covers!"

"Ruh-huh!" Scooby nodded and gulped. "Ret's go!"

"I think we should check in the alley." Velma explained, "Cats like to hang out there."

They looked under big cardboard boxes and in Dumpsters. They called Teddy's name softly. But suddenly, a window in the building next door flew open and a woman stuck out her head.

"Quiet!" she screeched. "I'm sick of all the comings and goings through that door at all hours of the day and night!"

"Hey, look!" Fred said as the woman slammed the window shut. "The factory door *is* open. Let's take a look inside. Teddy might have wandered in and gotten trapped."

The factory was a little spooky inside. Many of the puppets looked almost real in the moonlight.

"Let's split up," Fred said. "I'll go this way with Daphne and Velma. Shaggy, you check that way with Scooby-Doo."

But Shaggy and Scooby didn't want to split up. They were still worried about the guards' warning.

"You know," said Daphne, "this place hasn't been closed very long. I'll bet there's still food around here someplace."

"Why didn't you say so?" Shaggy cried cheerfully. "C'mon, Scooby, let's take a look around!"

"There's got to be a refrigerator around here someplace," Shaggy told Scooby as they searched the warehouse.

"Reah! Refrigerator!" Scooby said, sniffing for food.

"I wonder what happened to the owner of this place," Shaggy said. "Like, I heard he had to close down because he lost all his money gambling."

But before Scooby could answer, an eerie voice called out from a little stage nearby — a puppet stage!

"Ladies and gentlemen!" said the voice. "Presenting the hilarious and haunting Punch and Judy Show!"

The weird puppets on the little stage did a play. "Hoo-hoo! I'm going to get you!" warned one puppet, Mr. Punch. *Wham!* He hit a girl puppet on the head.

"Boo-hoo! I'm going to get you!" cried Judy, the other puppet. *Wham!* Judy hit Mr. Punch back.

The two puppets laughed and disappeared. Then, all of the sudden, a bunch of puppets popped up behind Shaggy and Scooby. Mr. Punch popped back up and pointed at them.

"No! no! no! I know what we'll do!" cackled Mr. Punch. "We're *haunted* puppets and we're going to get *you!*"

Scooby and Shaggy tried to get away, but the puppets followed close behind.

"Hee-hee-hee!" Mr. Punch laughed. "Look who I see!"

The puppets swung at Shaggy and Scooby with their little clubs. Shaggy and Scooby grabbed some empty paint cans and put them on their heads as helmets.

"Zoinks! Like, this bunch of haunted puppets has a burning desire to see us clubbed, Scoob!" Shaggy cried.

"Ri know! Ri know!" Scooby bellowed as they ran wildly through the warehouse.

Meanwhile, Fred and the girls were searching another area of the factory. Velma found an important clue on the floor.

"Look at this!" Velma said. "Paperwork for shipping puppet heads to Tahiti. It has today's date on it!"

Before Velma could say more, a spotlight came on, shining right in Fred's, Daphne's, and Velma's eyes. It was coming from a platform above, where a ventriloquist's dummy was sitting.

"Greetings," the dummy said, all by himself. "I'm afraid you've come to the wrong place at the wrong time!"

The talking dummy wasn't the gang's only surprise. Mrs. Jenkins' cat, Teddy, was sitting on its lap.

"Who are you?" asked Daphne. "What do you want?"

"I am the leader of the haunted puppets," the dummy said. "We turn anyone who comes into our warehouse into haunted puppets, too!"

"We don't believe in haunted puppets," Fred said. "Whatever you're up to, you won't get away with it!"

"We'll see about that!" The dummy laughed as he pulled a switch. Before Fred, Daphne, and Velma could get out of the way, a cage dropped from the ceiling and trapped them inside!

The dummy pulled a few more switches. Wires dropped from the ceiling. On the ends of the wires were claws that grabbed the gang by their arms and lifted them up into the air. The wires picked up and put down the gang over and over again, making their arms and legs dance wildly.

"Dance! Dance!" laughed the dummy. "Now you know how a puppet feels. Soon you will be a puppet, too, when I cast my haunting spell on you! Ha-ha-ha!"

Fred, Daphne, and Velma started to worry they might be dancing like that forever!

At the same time, Shaggy and Scooby-Doo were thinking they'd lost the creepy Mr. Punch and his crew. They were hiding in the costume room. But when they stopped to take a breath, Mr. Punch popped out at them again.

"Hee-hee-hee! You can't lose me!" giggled Mr. Punch. "I am Mr. Punch, you see?"

"Like, run, Scoob, run!" Shaggy cried.

"Ri am running!" Scooby yelped.

Shaggy and Scooby didn't know it, but they were heading right into the arms — or legs — of danger! Creepy spider puppets were coming for them!

Crash! Scooby-Doo and Shaggy collided with the huge spiders. They all fell to the ground in a pile.

"Help! Help!" Shaggy yelled. "These hairy horrors have me trapped in their web!"

"Ree too! Ree too!" cried Scooby.

Shaggy stopped kicking. "Hey, look, Scoob," he said. "These puppets aren't moving! I guess they're not the haunted kind."

"Roh, yeah," Scooby said, relieved.

Then they noticed, happily, that Mr. Punch had vanished.

But they didn't have much time to relax, because . . .

. . . a giant dragon puppet was headed straight for them!

It roared and breathed fire as it flew over their heads. Then it turned and swung back around, aiming right for Scoob and Shag!

Scooby and Shaggy ran — straight into a wall! Slowly, they turned around and looked right into the eyes of the ferocious dragon.

"Like, good-bye, ol' pal," said Shaggy. "I guess this dragon is going to have himself a Shaggy and Scooby-Doo barbecue!"

"Roh, noooooo!" Scooby cried and covered his eyes with his paws.

BOOOOOOSH! The dragon blew fire at them!

Meanwhile, the dummy had left Fred, Daphne, and Velma hanging from the wires. They could hear him laughing in the distance.

"We've got to find a way to get down from here," Fred said.

"I've got an idea," said Daphne. She reached around carefully and took off one of her shoes. Then she threw it toward the wall. The shoe hit one of the switches near the dummy's platform. In a split second, Fred was released from the wires.

"Good shot, Daphne!" Fred cheered. "I'll have you two down in no time."

"We've got to warn Shaggy and Scooby about that crazy dummy," Daphne said, once they were all free.

"Hey, I think I've found another clue," said Velma, looking at a puppet head she'd pulled from a crate. "This head has money stuffed inside it! Why would someone do that?"

Instead of an answer, the gang got a big surprise! Mr. Punch and some other puppets popped out from behind the crate.

"More visitors? Well, well, well!" Mr. Punch sneered. "We'll get them here and now, so they'll not tell!"

"Run, gang!" Fred yelled.

The gang quickly hurried away, leaving the puppets behind. Luckily, they escaped in the nick of time.

"You got away, tee-hee, tee-hee!" Mr. Punch cackled. "But we'll get you, wait and see!"

"What are we going to do now?" asked Velma.

"I think the answer is right in front of us," Fred said, pointing. "Look, it's Biff and Bob, the night watchmen. They'll help us."

The gang told the guards what they had seen. When they'd finished, the guards didn't answer. In fact, they didn't even move.

"What's wrong with them?" Daphne asked worriedly.

"I'll tell you," said a creepy voice from behind them.

When Fred, Daphne, and Velma turned around, they were face-to-face with the dummy, Mr. Punch, and their crew once more.

"We've turned them into puppets," said the dummy.

"Yes, indeed, indeedy do!" laughed Mr. Punch. "And now we'll turn you into puppets, too!"

Meanwhile, the dragon had almost caught up with Shaggy and Scooby. But before it could blast them with its fiery breath, they dropped to the ground and crawled under its belly. They ran with all their might, trying to lose the huge, beastly puppet.

Then, all at once, Shaggy and Scooby tripped over an old dummy lying on the ground. They flew through the air and landed in a rolling cart. The cart took off like a shot. It was moving so fast, they'd soon left the dragon far behind.

"Rook out!" Scooby cried. There was a lion in the cart! But it was just a puppet head. Scooby quickly tossed it away.

"Like, gangway!" Shaggy hollered as the cart zipped along.

Just as the dummy and his puppets were reaching for Fred, Daphne, and Velma, their friends Shaggy and Scooby raced by in the rolling cart.

"Like, anybody need a ride?" Shaggy cried.

Fred, Daphne, and Velma leaped into the cart. They all sped away from the angry puppets.

"Nice going, Shaggy and Scooby," Fred said as they all raced along. "I only have one question — how do we stop this thing?"

"I was afraid you were going to ask that!" said Shaggy.

"ROOOOOOH!" Scooby moaned.

Crash! The cart ran into a wall and tipped the whole gang onto the floor.

"Well, it was a bumpy way to escape, but I guess we're okay," Daphne said as they got to their feet.

"Never mind the bumps!" Shaggy said. "Look, snacks!"

"Roh boy, roh boy!" Scooby cheered.

"The machine's out of order. I'll just leave the money in the coin return," Shaggy explained, reaching his arm into the vending machine.

"Look at these pictures," Velma said. "Someone who worked here spends a lot of time on the beach."

COFFEE

Suddenly, the dragon appeared overhead and let out a scorching blast!

Shaggy wanted to run, but his hand was stuck! Scooby grabbed him and tugged with all his might. But Shaggy wouldn't budge.

"Zoinks! Pull, Scoob!" Shaggy begged. "Pull like you've never pulled before!"

"Ri'm pulling, ri'm pulling!" Scooby cried.

At last Shaggy's hand came free. He and Scooby stumbled backward, accidentally hitting a nearby switch.

All of a sudden, the dragon stopped. The gang looked up at it. It was just sitting still in midair.

"Look, it was just a puppet on a rail!" Daphne exclaimed.

"And the fire the dragon was breathing was probably created with some of these Chinese New Year fireworks," Velma added.

"I'm beginning to think those puppets aren't as haunted as they seem," Fred told them. "I think we should set a trap for them."

Fred had an idea how to distract the puppets. He wanted Scooby and Shaggy to dress up as acrobats, jump around, and wave sparklers in the air. When they got the attention of the puppets, Fred and the girls would sneak up on the puppets and surprise them.

"Like, no way, Fred!" said Shaggy. "I don't want to end up as a haunted puppet!"

"Ree, neither!" Scooby said.

"Would you do it for a Scooby Snack?" Velma pulled out a box. "They're double-butterscotch flavor!"

Moments later, Scooby-Doo and Shaggy were all dressed up and dancing around, sparklers in hand and paw. Sure enough, the haunted puppets were there in a flash.

"I don't know what game you're playing," the dummy puppet leader said angrily, "but the time has come to lock you up and turn you into puppets!"

"Like, I think the time has come for us to run away," Shaggy said nervously. "Are you with me, Scoob?"

"Ruh-uh." Scooby shook his head. "Ri'm in front of you!"

Just as Scooby and Shaggy started to flee, three policemen appeared out of nowhere.

"Everybody freeze!" shouted one of the policemen.

"Everybody run!" shouted the dummy.

Teddy the cat, who had been sitting quietly nearby, was frightened by all the noise. He jumped right on Scooby's head. Scooby tripped and fell toward the box of fireworks. Shaggy tried to catch Scooby and Teddy, but he went tumbling, too.

As they fell, one of the sparklers fell into the box of fireworks. It lit a fuse, and . . .

Boom! Bang! Blam!

The fireworks went off, exploding in colorful lights and patterns all over the factory.

"Don't shoot! Don't shoot!" someone yelled. "We give up!"

A bunch of men ran out from behind the boxes and crates. They all had enormous puppets on their hands.

"We confess!" said a man with the dummy on his arm. "We're the bank robbers! We did it!"

"All right! Don't move!" said one of the policemen. "Shaggy, tie up these criminals!"

"There, all tied up and prison-bound!" said Shaggy when he had finished the last knot. "But how do you cops know my name?"

"Because we're not really policemen," Fred said as he, Daphne, and Velma stood up, holding the policemen in their arms. "These are puppets. We found them in the costume room, and we realized they'd be perfect for tricking whoever was working the haunted puppets."

"The two guards are actually puppets," Velma explained. "The haunted puppets are really the bank robbers, the owner of this factory and his men. They were going to smuggle all the money they'd stolen out of the country and live in the tropics."

"They made up the haunted puppet story to keep people away while they robbed banks," Daphne said as the real police took the robbers away.

"We would have gotten away with our plan, too, if it weren't for you pesky kids and that dog!" growled the owner of the puppet factory.

"Just think, we solved another mystery *and* returned Teddy to Mrs. Jenkins," Fred said.

Mrs. Jenkins was overjoyed. "I'm the happiest woman in town, thanks to you kids!"

Shaggy smiled. "And no strings attached, thanks to Scooby-Doo!"

"Rooby-Dooby-Doo!" cheered Scooby-Doo.

FUN TIME PUPPET CO.